TEEN TITANS GO!™

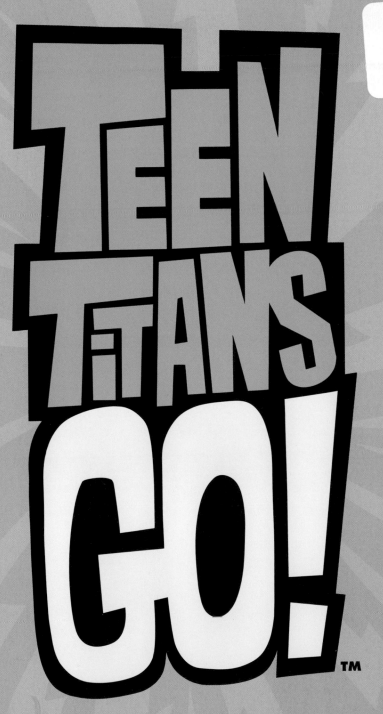

Little, Brown and Company

Hachette Book Group
1290 Avenue of the Americas, New York, NY 10104
Visit us at lb-kids.com

First Edition: May 2017

Little, Brown and Company is a division of Hachette Book Group, Inc. The Little, Brown and Company name and logo are trademarks of Hachette Book Group, Inc.

The publisher is not responsible for websites (or their content) that are not owned by the publisher.

Library of Congress Control Number 2016952268

ISBNs: 978-0-316-54809-0 (pbk.), 978-0-316-54808-3 (ebook), 978-0-316-55356-8 (ebook), 978-0-316-55358-2 (ebook)

Printed in the United States of America

CW

10 9 8 7 6 5 4 3 2 1

TEEN TITANS GO!

BABY BIRD BLUES

Adapted by Jonathan Evans

Based on the episode "Hose Water"

written by Ben Gruber

LITTLE, BROWN AND COMPANY

New York   Boston

Inside Titans Tower, Beast Boy is playing a video game when Cyborg bursts in, more amped up than usual. "Stop what you are doing immediately *and look at me!*" he says.

Beast Boy doesn't need to be told twice. "I'm looking, brah!"

"Ready for the most amazing sight ever?" Cyborg asks excitedly.

Cyborg can barely contain himself and puts out his hand. He's holding a baby bird!

Beast Boy is confused. "Is it hiding behind the bird?"

"It *is* the bird! Isn't nature amazing?" Cyborg replies.

"No, brah. Not amazing. At all." Beast Boy goes back to his game, completely unimpressed. Cyborg is sad, but he's determined to find someone who thinks his bird is awesome.

Meanwhile, Raven is enjoying her solitude when Starfire approaches her, even more enthusiastic than usual. And she's normally *very* enthusiastic. "Dearest Friend Raven, I must show you something wondrous! Look!"

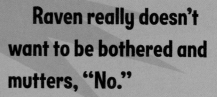

Raven really doesn't want to be bothered and mutters, "No."

Starfire ignores her. "Behold the object of beauty." She holds out a brightly colored egg.

Raven is *totally* unimpressed. "You made me open my lids for a shell?"

"Don't the colors bring you joy?" asks Starfire.

Raven is filled with the opposite of joy. "I *hate* colorful things," she says bitterly, wishing she could meditate uninterrupted.

Starfire and Cyborg are annoyed. But when they run into each other, Starfire exclaims, "Look at that cutest of baby birds you are holding! Chirp! Chirp!"

The bird chirps back. Cyborg giggles, then he gasps. "I think that's the shell this little guy hatched from!"

Suddenly, Starfire realizes something. "The birds hatch out of the eggs?"

"Well, not *all* eggs," Cyborg replies.

Starfire is determined. *"We must free the imprisoned birdies!"*

Cyborg and Starfire raid the refrigerator and take out a carton of eggs. Starfire grabs one and exclaims, "Be free, tiny bird!" She smashes it on the floor.

Cyborg grabs another one and shouts, "Freedom!"

They smash every last egg, but no birds escape. They're very relieved that none of the eggs were secretly holding little birds prisoner.

Robin—leader of the Titans, egg-lover, and all-around busybody—is also in the kitchen. He is mortified by the egg massacre. "*Stop!* You're destroying nature's best source of protein and puns!" he screams.

Raven and Beast Boy walk in.

"What's with all the *egg*-citement?" Raven asks.

Robin is jealous of Raven's pun and says, "Cyborg and Starfire are *egging* each other on."

"Well played," Raven grumbles.

"We're just having the bird fun, Robin," Starfire explains.

"And the breaking-stuff fun, too!" Cyborg adds.

"Let us break more of the objects!" says Starfire.

"What? No!" shouts Robin.
Too late. Starfire and Cyborg are already committed to wrecking stuff.

They go through Titans Tower and break everything they can get their hands on.

Afterward, they build a fort and have tea.

"Stop acting like children!" Robin shouts.

"Why?" Cyborg asks. "We're just having innocent fun. Like trying to find the end of the rainbow, or that nursery rhyme about the woman who lives in a giant shoe."

"That rhyme is most wondrous," Starfire says.

"But there's a reason we leave childish things behind," warns the frustrated Robin.

Cyborg gasps in surprise. "What is it?"

"I can't tell you. But the consequences will be highly *eggs*-treme."

"But we *like* having the exuberance of the children," Starfire says, running off with Cyborg.

And like that, the two friends are off to roll down hills, blow bubbles, marvel at bugs, and paint their faces.

When Robin sees the face paint, he can't take it anymore. He tackles both Cyborg and Starfire.

"I know things about face paint. It's dangerous. I was a tiger once!" he yells in a panic, remembering how close he once came to having that kind of childlike fun.

Robin wipes off the paint. Something isn't right. "Your faces. They're different! Everything looks...younger."

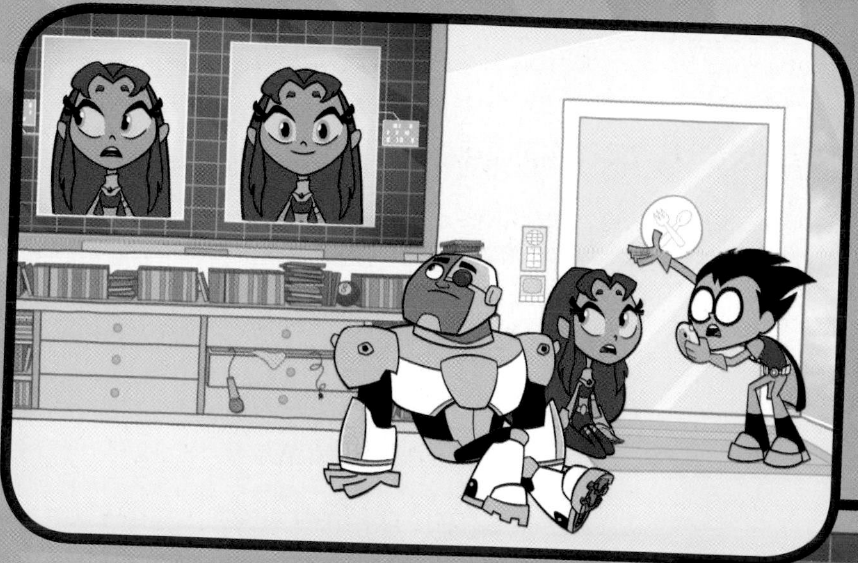

"Look!" he continues. "Compare your faces *now* to the way they looked just eight hours ago."

"Oh, Robin. We just *feel* younger," explains Cyborg, not really seeing a difference.

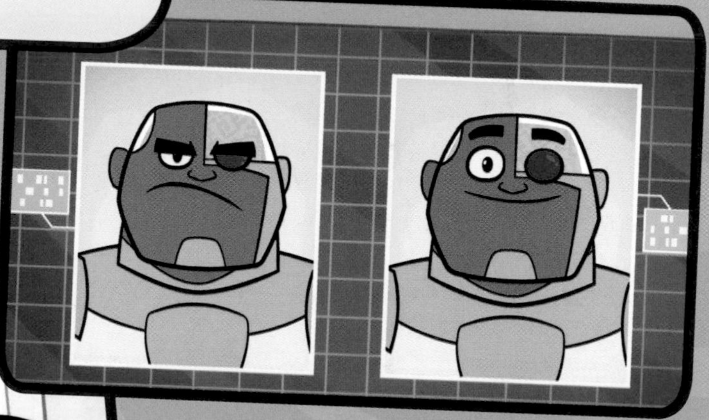

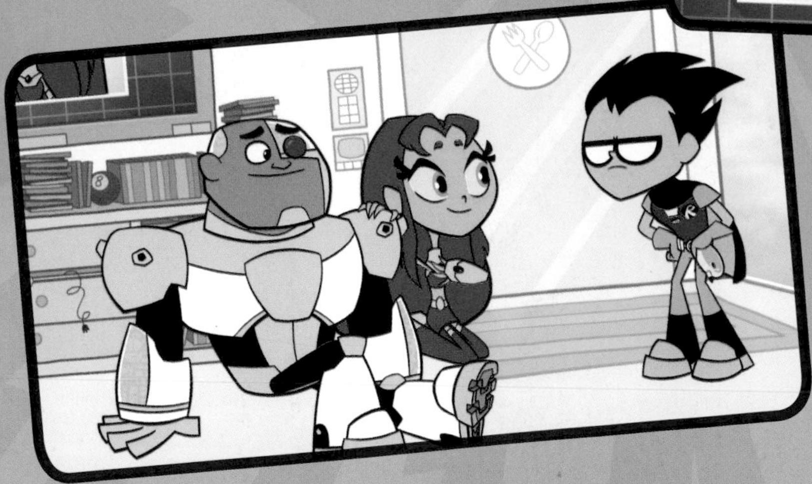

"Now, we'd love to look at more boring pictures with you, but we're gonna go drink water from the hose."

Raven and Beast Boy want to know what the ruckus is all about. "All this noise is *egg*-ravating," puns Raven.

"Starfire and Cyborg are toying with forces they don't understand." Robin complains.

"They're just playing hide-and-seek, dude," says Beast Boy, who's a little confused about why Robin's stressing out.

"*Eggs*-actly." Robin replies, turning and looking at Cyborg and Starfire suspiciously.

Robin explains that if they aren't stopped, Cyborg and Starfire will keep getting younger and younger until—*POOF*! They all hear a strange sound...

Cyborg and Starfire have de-aged so much, they've turned into eggs!

"You know what this means?" Robin asks no one in particular.

"Yes," Raven answers. "More egg puns."

Beast Boy sees a stork enter the room. "Oh, snap! It's the pickle bird."

"That's not the pickle bird," Robin says. "That's the bird in charge of bringing babies."

But the stork is not dropping off any babies or pickles. He's there to collect the eggs formerly known as Cyborg and Starfire!

Robin has to rescue his egg-friends from the stork! "Sorry, but we don't serve breakfast after eleven. *Titans, go!*"

Robin, Beast Boy, and Raven hop into the Titans Jet and chase the stork to a place of hope, discovery, and dreams— the place where babies come from.

"I know it looks all fun and innocent, but if we want to get our friends back," Robin says, "*we have to destroy it all!*"

Robin gives a pep talk as they parachute in: "We can do this, Titans. Just pretend you're an adult with a mortgage."

They lay waste to the paradise. At least until Beast Boy discovers a giant shoe house and starts to de-age. "So *cool*! Look how big those laces are!"

"The optimism is too strong!" Robin yells as Beast Boy transforms into an egg.

Several bugs close in. "What now?" Raven asks.

"We act our age! Remember, bugs are not fascinating! They're disgusting creatures! Right, Raven?"

But Raven thinks the bugs are neat, and she transforms.

Robin is by himself and beside himself. "Don't give up! We can still be sad, lonely adults!" But then he spots the stork painting an egg.

Robin can't help it. "The colors. Must... resist...temptation."

But he can't. The colors, the joy, it's just too much. "So bright! *I want to be a tiger!*" he says, and he transforms.

"Well," the stork says, "I wasn't *eggs*-pecting this. You see that? *I'm the egg-pun guy!*"

THE END.

WILL THE TITANS EVER RE-AGE TO FIGHT CRIME ONCE MORE???